An offer too good to refuse, but at what cost?

One last surprise waited for Betty: an application to qualify as a contractor for the Baron County Police Department. Specifically, to re-examine evidence from recent crime scenes. A background check, a confidentiality agreement, and…an offer of payment.

"Wow," Betty whispered, shaking her head.

Payment equal to what she'd earned over the last six months of work her lab assistants could do in their sleep.

Turning Detective Willa Belladeux down cold didn't seem nearly as easy as it had the night before, but not because of the money.

Well, not *only* because of the money.

The feeling of being in demand, of being appreciated, carried a lot more weight and influence. The idea of getting to work in the field she'd wanted. Yes, what she'd trained for. What her talents and skills were best suited for.

All of that together got Betty up and dialing the number on the business card clipped to the application before she could change her mind.

DNA Never Lies:

Bending the Code ∞ Book One

Copyright © 2020 by Kari A. Kilgore

All rights reserved

Published 2020 by Spiral Publishing, Ltd.
www.spiralpublishing.net
St. Paul, Virginia

Book and cover design copyright © 2020 by Spiral Publishing, Ltd.

Cover art copyright © 2020 by MassimoVernicesole |
depositphotos.com

ISBN-13: 978-1-948890-42-7
Large Print ISBN-13: 978-1-948890-45-8

Library of Congress Control Number: 2020932289

This book is licensed for your personal enjoyment only. All rights
reserved. is is a work of fiction. All characters and events portrayed in
this book are fictional, and any resemblance to real people or incidents is
purely coincidental. This book, or parts thereof, may not be reproduced
in any form without permission.

For Joyce

Who can always imagine an alternate scenario

DNA NEVER LIES

BENDING THE CODE ∞ BOOK ONE

KARI KILGORE

SPIRAL PUBLISHING, LTD.

Chapter 1

WHY DID the boring jobs always pay the best?

Betty Falconen leaned back in her rickety rolling lab chair, far enough to get a good stretch but not enough to dump herself on the faded pea-green tile floor. Again.

Everyone else had long gone home for the weekend, so she had her tiny lab in all its dubious glory to herself. Antique florescent light fixture in the corner that blinked no matter how many times they changed the bulb. The squat dorm-style refrigerator covered with rust circles from distant college beers past, complete with strange clanky noise. The row of tall lab bench tables with clean but chipped and stained white plastic surfaces.

At least the office surplus shop across town hadn't charged Betty for those.

Janie's Second Chance Office Emporium was struggling, just like Betty was, but Jane wasn't desperate enough to charge someone to haul off her junk. Especially junk donated from the biology department at Georgia Tech that no one but Betty would want.

Betty sat up, her scuffed black tennis shoes hitting the

floor with a flat smack. She tilted her head to the side, brushing her wavy dark hair away from her round granny reading glasses. A low gronk, too quiet for anyone not quite so neurotically observant to notice, sounded again from the matte black sequencer workstation hunched under her desk like a gargoyle.

Sure enough, one of the machine's cooling fans was about to go on the fritz, and just in time for the mortgage on this office to come due. Janice, her low-rent IT guru, kept telling her to yank this place kicking and screaming out of the 2020s and upgrade the equipment already. Easy for her to say.

A hell of a lot easier to *do* back before everyone and their auntie decided they were genetics experts. Just because testing was so cheap nowadays didn't mean the results were worth a damn. At least not if you couldn't understand them.

Betty leaned toward the hulking black cube, almost close enough to rest her ear against the surface. At nearly three feet on each side, the biggest problem with the sequencer would be moving the silly thing so Janice could check it out. A warm plastic smell wafted up, but it wasn't to the burning red alert panic stage just yet.

If the antiquated solid state monstrosity could just get this batch of DNA samples processed and cross-matched, Betty promised herself she'd get the new photonic drives Janice kept mentioning. Not very subtly, either.

The gronks settled down, allowing Betty to mentally walk back that promise a bit.

Soon. She'd upgrade everything soon.

This overflow work for the wildlife services from more than one state along the Eastern seaboard was about as exciting as watching a centrifuge spin, but the states paid on time. Figuring out if the latest big cat capture qualified for federal funding wasn't exactly the kind of exotic puzzle solving Betty daydreamed about during her college days.

Before it all went bad, she thought she'd be out there in the middle of the action, maybe tracking the Big Bads, or even the big cats, herself.

A steady supply of this kind of mundane but plentiful work sure could help pay the bills around this joint, though. Bills that included the convenience of trudging upstairs to her not quite so shabby apartment when she was finished rather than commuting to an equally dreary apartment she could afford. Which would mean far, far away from Atlanta's city limits.

After a couple of minutes of gronk-free processing, Betty felt safe enough to lean back again. She frowned as she picked up her stainless steel coffee tankard. Way too light, so obviously way too empty.

Rows of narrow test tubes waited on the desk beside her, every one filled with drops of blood from cougars or panthers or whatever they were calling them these days. She wasn't going to get early completion bonuses on these contracts and earn favored-contractor status for more by punking out early and heading upstairs.

Well, working at nine o'clock on a Friday evening might not seem early to most, but most didn't have Betty's bills to deal with.

She could still taste the foul, overcooked sludge the office machine grudgingly spit out in the back of her throat. Overcooked budget or not, a night like this called for desperate measures.

Betty pulled out her cracked smartphone to place an order from the expensive hipster coffee shop down the block. The staff annoyed her almost as much as the ads on every other website and TV show these days, trumpeting how fast and cheap you could solve the mysteries of your own DNA and cure all your ills and even find your perfect mate with only a drop or two of spit.

The coffee was fantastic, though.

Even better, the app saved her from having to actually speak to anyone, since no one who worked there was likely to do more than grunt when Betty picked up her order.

One more glance at the aged and badly in need of retirement sequencer, a quick investigation of her pockets to make sure she had enough cash, and Betty headed out into the early evening.

Even well away from any sort of excitement or nightlife, the street wasn't the least bit dangerous after dark. It was way too dull for that. Just a row of ordinary red brick buildings that probably didn't even seem stylish or new when they were built decades ago around the end of the last century. Only a couple of the ground-level offices stood empty, and they wouldn't for long.

The rest were full of accountants and lawyers who couldn't afford the rent in the skyscrapers downtown, office supply stores with mostly new stuff for people who could afford such things, and a couple of mediocre delis and lunch places locked up tight for the night.

The streetlights kept everything bright enough to feel safe but not so well illuminated that it would be depressing. The rows of cars lined up more or less within the boundaries of the parking meters were in decent enough shape. Mostly more than five years old, but less than fifteen, with no gas-powered clunkers fighting the outdated fight against the electric car revolution. Clean, but nowhere flashy enough for any self-respecting thief to take a second look.

Not that any self-respecting thief would be caught down here on a bet.

Betty breathed in the crisp October air, several blocks

away from the interstate, so relatively free of the exhaust still spewed by those surviving gas clunkers. Even though her brain felt almost as noisy and ill-maintained as her favorite sequencer after weeks of these kinds of routine jobs, she had to admit getting out and walking around helped.

She made yet another in a series of promises to herself to do more of this and start taking better care of herself before what passed for winter in Atlanta really settled in.

A couple of blocks down, the lights overhead brightened up and so did the general atmosphere of the neighborhood. Nothing too trendy or expensive. That was still several blocks on toward the university. But enough to have modest crowds wandering and eating and shopping.

Maybe not people who couldn't afford to go to the latest hot spot, like Betty. But those who were smart enough to avoid those hotspots on purpose.

She turned left and nearly walked right into a shiny metal fence that hadn't been there the last time she made this late-night coffee run a couple of weeks ago. A brand new restaurant had sprung up out of the concrete sidewalk like they tended to do around here. A collection of tiny little round tables somehow managed to hold color-changing lights, angular metal vases full of flowers made of various kinds of wire, and miniature plates of colorful food that likely cost a fortune.

The young people sprawled around the space all looked like they would soon get up and wander back into the pages of the edgy fashion holo-zines they'd escaped from. All asymmetrical hair and rather adventurous clothing and pale, carefully bored faces.

Betty felt an uncharacteristic burst of self-consciousness at her typical work uniform of baggy black pants, an oversized t-shirt, and hair that had last seen a brush dragged through it hours ago.

On the other hand, she seemed more or less invisible to these people, which suited her just fine.

She dodged around the fence and kept heading for her coffee.

The shop was two doors down, past a bookstore that stubbornly refused to carry any variety of holo-novel, which Betty heartily approved of. She wasn't willing to shell out for the fancy reader, for one thing. And she still loved the feel and smell of a printed book, thank you very much.

A huge stylized bright blue cup of very dark coffee complete with steam wafting up projected itself from Betty's destination, looking and smelling realistic enough to pick up and take home. The Bean had no problems embracing new technology in their advertising, but thank goodness they roasted and ground up their beans the old fashioned way.

The much stronger coffee aroma inside woke Betty up almost enough that she could have skipped her dose. But not quite enough for her to do it.

The crowd inside the bare-brick-and-exposed-ductwork space wasn't too bad, not for a weekend night. A few clusters of young people with their noses buried in computers or holo-books clearly belonged to the university. A group of women laughing loud enough to make Betty's ears hurt surely were coming from or heading to some bar or other.

All typical for The Bean.

Another woman closer to Betty's age, sitting at a table by herself without a book or computer or even a phone in sight, wasn't typical at all. She even sipped from a reusable water bottle rather than from anything caffeinated.

Short-cropped brown hair standing on end, too irregular to be anything but the result of an absent-minded person running her hands through it. A rumpled button-up brown shirt with slacks to match. And a sharp, angular face and piercing blue eyes that obviously didn't miss a single thing that happened anywhere close by.

Betty glanced at the strange woman again, somehow not surprised to to find her looking back. Betty nodded once, then stepped up to the pickup counter.

No matter what the stranger's story was, all Betty wanted was to get her portable caffeine buzz, get back to work, and get the next set of samples going. With any luck, she'd be finished and upstairs and asleep before anyone in this coffee shop made it home.

Meaning before dawn, pretty much.

Before Betty could manage to catch the attention of the jittery baristas, a cool voice spoke from beside her.

"I got it, Ms. Falconen."

Chapter 2

Betty knew who would be standing there before she turned around.

The odd woman with the messy hair.

"Thanks, but that's not necessary," Betty said, hoping her smile looked somewhat friendly but didn't cross the line into welcoming the intrusion. "Just gonna grab it and go."

The part of Betty's brain that had been feeling bored silly and stifled and trapped since these dreadfully routine contracts started perked up more than a vat of coffee could manage.

A *stranger?* Who knew her *name?* And knew she'd be *here* tonight?

How exciting!

The rest of her wanted nothing more than to avoid any sort of hassle and get back to work.

"I insist," the stranger said. Before Betty could intercept, the woman flashed her smart phone at the glowing charging station on the counter. Once the light changed from red to green, the baristas knew they didn't even have to interrupt their high-speed conversations for something as antiquated as processing a cash payment.

Betty wished she could ignore the woman now standing right in front of her just as easily.

"Thanks," she said, grabbing the warm cup. "Late night for me. See you around."

"Ms. Falconen, I only need a minute of your time right now."

Betty froze mid-dash, too intrigued to resist even though all the excuses in the world were flooding through her mind.

Not in a dating mood lately with men or women. Don't have time for dating. Can't possibly afford dating.

Can't even afford friendship, not a new one. No interest in meeting anyone new, for any reason.

And the most true and effective: way too tired for any of this nonsense, whatever it turns out to be.

The intrigued side won out, as usual.

"I don't think I remember you. Have we met?"

The stranger shook her head before she jerked her chin toward the table.

"We haven't, not yet. Willa Belladeux, Baron County Police."

Willa Bella-do. Nice musical ring to it. Betty couldn't quite override her curiosity and make her escape despite her lack of interest in getting mixed up with law enforcement.

"I'm pretty sure you have the wrong person," she said, sitting with her back to the room. Her absolute least favorite place to sit in *any* room. "I'm just a private scientist, not working in a crime lab or anything like that."

Willa nodded. "That's exactly why I came out here, Betty. I don't even have jurisdiction out here in Fulton, remember? Not flashing a badge, either. I'm just here to talk."

"Talk then. But not for too long. I have a bunch of samples running."

"The wildlife samples, right? Cats, I believe."

Betty sat back and crossed her arms.

"I don't know whether to point out that my work is none of your business or ask how the hell you know that."

Willa took a long sip of her water.

"Those assignments, the wildlife ones, are none of my business. You're right about that. I'm a good detective is how I know that. You're not exactly working up to your level, are you?"

Betty let out her breath in a rush, turning to the side. How had this Willa person known exactly where to hit her like that? The same sore spot she'd been digging at herself not fifteen minutes earlier.

"I'm working just fine, thanks. Speaking of work, I really do need to get back. So if this is all you got, thanks for the coffee, but I'm out."

"I need your help, Betty."

The quiet tone got Betty's attention a lot more than the words did. Quiet, and…pleading.

"Then start making sense instead of telling me how I'm wasting my education or some other such nonsense."

Willa nodded, stared up at the ceiling for several seconds, then focused on Betty and started talking.

"I'm working a string of robberies. Before you argue, hear me out. All of this is public record. These aren't a simple case of smash and grab, unsolved because the thief didn't leave a trace we could follow. These are several high-end buildings out in Maplehurst and Baron, real nice places. Top of the line all the way. Golf, tennis, swimming pools. Solar panels everywhere. Super efficient smart

HVAC. They even have their own CommuShare stations, most of them."

"So you're saying that sort of thing doesn't happen in this sort of place, right?"

"You got it. But that's only part of the problem. The security is high-end, too. Cameras, retina ID, 24/7 surveillance. And no one is breaching it. Not in the units that got hit or anywhere else."

"Okay, that's strange. Still, why me?"

Willa waved one hand toward Betty, palm up.

"DNA testing is proving to be a problem. The only traces we're finding in the apartments that got robbed matches the residents. No exceptions so far. All of them swear they didn't lose their own stuff, which I understand. Hard to imagine they'd all be working together in some kind of organized scheme to defraud their insurance agencies. Then this past week, the whole thing escalated."

"What, the landlord finally get hit?"

Willa shook her head, her face serious enough that Betty settled down her next few smartass remarks.

"Not exactly. One of the tenants, one who'd been robbed before, was attacked. Sexually assaulted. Murdered."

Betty closed her eyes for several seconds, swallowing a few times. And here she'd been cracking jokes. Willa went on.

"This bit isn't exactly public record, but it will likely get out soon enough. Testing showed no trace of DNA except the victim's and her boyfriend of the last eight years. No evidence or reports of trouble between them, and the guy was absolutely gutted. But with no evidence of anyone else, he's in lockup. Makes no sense, but that's what we got."

"And you don't believe it."

"No, Betty, I do not. See, I've had the misfortune to

investigate a lot of murders and sexual assaults over the years. Her boyfriend wasn't acting his response, I'd stake my career on it. I don't care what the evidence showed in this case. It wasn't him. I know there's almost always something, some trace left behind. But we can't find it. None of this fits."

"Except the DNA that was left behind," Betty said. "Which doesn't lie."

That hand wave again. Then both of Willa's hands scrubbed through her hair, just like Betty suspected.

"Doesn't it, Betty? *Ever?* There's got to be something here."

"I'm sorry to disappoint you, Willa, but no. It doesn't. That's one boring part about the work. What I've been doing lately, anyway. As long as the sample is sound and I do my job, the answer is pretty clear cut. In a case like this, the odds of someone else randomly matching are too astronomical to be worth considering. This guy may not have murdered his girlfriend, no. But with what you've got so far, it makes sense to investigate him. I'm sorry."

Willa took a deep breath and let it out slowly. Her being a detective explained the way she struck Betty as watchful and observant. Willa Belladeux probably rarely, if ever, missed anything.

Then why was she so convinced everyone *else* was missing something here?

"Okay, I'll bite," Betty said. "What is it you're asking me to do?"

"I checked your background already. You're squeaky clean, if a bit underwhelming with your choices of work. I say I ask you about that. You answer in a way I can live with. Then I clear you with the department to re-examine the evidence."

"Hang on, you're not making sense. What made this

seem worth checking into me before you even talked to me? I'm so standard I bore myself."

Willa smiled, and the effect was like clouds parting to reveal a brilliant, sunny day.

"You said it earlier. 'As long as the sample is sound and I do my job.' You're way too damn smart and talented to be toiling away for next to no money in a second-rate private lab. What got you into this instead of better opportunities?"

Betty glanced around even though she knew no one was listening. Well, she thought no one was listening. With her back to the damn room, she had no real way to tell.

"I got the work I could get. That's all. The lab most certainly is second-rate, on the surface at least. But it's mine, and we do top-rate work. I'm not sure what you think I can do except re-run the analysis and get the same results."

"You can do what you were *trained* to do, Ms. Falconen. You weren't any standard student, undergrad, postgrad, none of it. You were drawn to the cutting-edge of forensic genetics from the start, I'd say past it and past the bleeding-edge, too. I won't say I understand much of what I read about you, not the hard-core science parts. But I understand you ran circles around your professors every step of the way."

Betty nodded once, then finished her coffee in one too-long, too-hot gulp.

"I ran circles around them, all right. Ran my own ass right out of the field and transformed into the glamorous specimen of mediocrity you see before you for my trouble. I might be able to refer you to someone who can help you. But I can't."

Before she could get to her feet, Willa grabbed her arm and spoke in an urgent, low voice.

"You can help me catch whoever *is* doing this before they strike again. Figure out how the hell they're managing to get in and out like a damn ghost. Make the bad person stop. Isn't that worth getting over a nasty incident that happened almost twenty years ago? And maybe you get the side benefit of finally doing the work you were *made* to do?"

In that second, the curiosity in Betty's heart and mind shivered and gave up.

Some might call it cowardice. She called it self-preservation.

In any case, she'd had enough.

Betty reached down and removed Willa's hand from her arm, leaned forward until she was only inches away, and put as much cold strength as she could manage into her glare.

"I don't know where you get your information, Detective Belladeux, but you're on the wrong path here. I hope you catch whoever this is. But you'll have to catch them without me."

Betty turned and walked out of The Bean without a backward glance.

Chapter 3

A LONGER THAN even she'd planned night of work combined with a restless, pretty much useless few hours of sleep left Betty grumpier than usual the next morning. Much as she could have used the help in the lab, she was thankful it was Saturday.

Having to deal with her snappish attitude would have sent her two underpaid assistants and probably the part-time secretary running for the streets before the shitty office coffee got cold.

The only saving grace was Betty was free to putter around in her pajamas all day long if she wanted to. The bright pink cotton pants and t-shirt might not be all that different from her work uniform, save for the much brighter color. It was comforting all the same.

She treated herself to a big mug of her own coffee, brewed upstairs in her apartment using supplies she was far too cheap—and too broke—to bring in down here. She didn't dare during the week. Too much chance of one of her underlings noticing how much better it smelled.

Probably noticing how Betty closed her eyes and

smiled after taking a sip rather than the sneering grimace the office brew demanded, too.

Her so-called sleep hadn't given her a break from the weird conversation with Detective Belladeux all night long. Or from what the detective had called a "nasty incident" that Betty should have simply been able to get over.

Those gut-wrenching, horrifying days right before she'd finally gotten her masters degree and ran played over and over again, waking her up in a cold sweat enough times that she finally gave up and got up.

Betty resolved to put the naïve detective and her own bad judgment in years gone by firmly out of her mind for the day. Even groggy, and grumpy, she could wrap up this latest batch of wildlife testing in record time.

Her resolve lasted until she stepped into the outer office to see how the day was going to shape up without her participation. The broad security glass window revealed a satisfyingly gray and windy morning, as it turned out. Betty's favorite kind of weather for being outside.

Too bad staying in her pajamas was mandatory today.

She groaned at a scatter of envelopes and paper across the pea-green tiles just inside the front door. Of all the damned old-fashioned things for an office in downtown Atlanta to have, the mail slot was probably Betty's least favorite. At least right now. She didn't much think about it when Jimmy was here to deal with it.

She carefully parked her coffee on Jimmy's suspiciously neat desk, squatted with a grunt, and swept the pile into her hands. Her first thought was to dump it all on the desk. If nothing else for the childish and temporary satisfaction of making a mess.

But even in her current belligerent mood, Betty didn't want to be quite *that* petulant.

Everything addressed to BNF Laboratories went into

the empty black metal IN box instead. Probably a depressing number of them were bills, and therefore technically Betty's problem. She was still trying to figure out why a few utilities and associations and such flat-out insisted on paper rather than email. Jimmy knew the weird procedures for paying those bills, even if he didn't always know how razor-thin the budget actually was around here.

Junk mail and neighborhood crap went straight into the bright green recycle bin, along with Betty's usual muttered questions about why people insisted on leaving the stuff here. She'd told them over and over again exactly where it would end up.

That left only a heavy magazine-sized envelope addressed directly to her.

No return address, no postage. Again, who were these people who insisted on sending paper?

In this case, probably someone who didn't want to *send* anything.

Maybe someone who walked right up to the door, bold as hell, and pushed it through the blasted letter slot.

Betty considered dumping it unopened on top of the rest of the recycling. Or better yet, into the break room trash can that ended up with all the damp garbage.

But either one of those risked someone else getting curious and opening it. The end of her academic career might have been the worst humiliation of her life so far, but Betty could think of a few more incidents she'd rather not have shared around the lab.

She glanced out at the street again, surprised when she didn't see Willa Belladeux staring back in at her, then headed back into the lab. She sat in her usual creaky office chair, noticing how the ancient black cube on the floor was processing gronk-free today.

Then Betty opened the envelope.

Rather than the mortifying details of her own life, several clippings and printouts from the *Maplehurst Post* slid out into her lap. She plopped the whole thing on one of the empty lab benches so she could see it all at once.

No doubt who'd sent or delivered the envelope.

Small articles about the robberies Detective Belladeux had mentioned, getting a bit longer each time as the previous ones were mentioned. And like she'd mentioned, all of them happened at the high-end apartment buildings over in Maplehurst.

Then a much bigger article about the most recent crime. The sexual assault and murder of one Rhonda Johnson had more ink, but nowhere near as many details of the crime itself. Thank goodness.

All of the articles mentioned how DNA samples had matched with residents of each apartment, much to the disgust and protest of the robbery victims.

The fact that all of the evidence around and on the murder victim was either her boyfriend's or her own hadn't made the paper at all.

Willa Belladeux had been honest about that much. With the exception of the strange lack of evidence at the murder scene, everything she'd told Betty was actually public record.

One last surprise waited under the articles: an application to qualify as a contractor for the Baron County Police Department. Specifically, to re-examine evidence from recent crime scenes. A background check, a confidentiality agreement, and…an offer of payment.

"Wow," Betty whispered, shaking her head.

Payment equal to what she'd earned over the last six months of work her lab assistants could do in their sleep.

Turning Willa Belladeux down cold didn't seem nearly

as easy as it had the night before, but not because of the money.

Well, not *only* because of the money.

The feeling of being in demand, of being appreciated, carried a lot more weight and influence. The idea of getting to work in the field she'd wanted. Yes, what she'd trained for. What her talents and skills were best suited for.

All of that together got Betty up and dialing the number on the business card clipped to the application before she could change her mind.

Turned out Willa wanted to make damn sure Betty knew who was behind this whole crazy thing. No guessing required.

Chapter 4

Rather than heading back over to The Bean or having to drive out to Maplehurst, Betty insisted on meeting at her own lab. If she was going into this strange situation where she'd be constantly behind and asking questions, at least this first part would happen on her own terms. On her own turf, even.

She did reluctantly go back upstairs to change clothes.

Two hours after Betty found the envelope, she and Willa sat around the small oval table in the all-beige-and-white break room, surrounded by brown paper bags that had once been full of take-out. That was the other condition for this meeting. Lunch from Ron-San's, the sushi place over in Maplehurst that Betty absolutely adored.

Thankfully Willa was more than happy to oblige, and to join Betty in the decadent feast.

Willa's hair didn't have quite the rumpled look of the night before at The Bean, but her clothes were considerably more relaxed. Her gray t-shirt and sweatpants weren't that far off from what Betty had changed into.

She'd also brought a thick blue metal briefcase that

Betty was reluctant to ask about. Though if the contents were related to the crimes, especially the last one, it might have been better to have a look before they ate.

Betty took a long sip of her warm green tea, then popped a bundle of white rice wrapped in black seaweed and topped with huge orange spheres of salmon roe into her mouth. She closed her eyes as the salty essence-of-salmon burst against her tongue. If she ate one more thing, she'd either be miserably full or sound asleep in less than an hour.

Time to focus, whether she wanted to or not.

"Okay, thank you for lunch," she said. "That was exactly what I needed. I have a feeling you have things you think I need to see in that big briefcase."

Willa nodded, still chewing her mouthful of sweetened scrambled egg and rice. Betty always saved her own tamago for last.

"I promised my boss I'd make you sign the contract before I let you take a look. Like I told you last night, nothing showed up on your background check. And your training and academic background speak for themselves. So the paperwork is nothing more than a formality. But my boss is…rather formal."

Betty shrugged, then retrieved the stack of papers from the chair beside her.

She'd filled everything out before Willa arrived.

"Fair enough. I'm not especially formal myself, but I'm used to dealing with people who are. I'll tell you one more time that I'm not sure what I can add that your internal folks haven't already done. I promise my equipment is older than even the county has."

"Maybe. Good thing I'm not looking for someone with brand new equipment. If I was, I'd be over at the university. What I need is fresh but not inexperienced eyes. And a mind that changed the course of forensic genetics while you were still in grad school."

Betty snorted. "I'm not so sure I changed anything. Changed my own course for damn sure, at least."

Willa sat back in her chair and crossed her arms.

"The woman who kicked the ability to sort out useful DNA from a jumbled up mixed sample from someday to right now? I'd say that was a major shift."

Betty shook her head, not wanting her pleasantly full stomach to start churning.

"Years ago won't help with what you're wanting me to try to do now. Do you have enough DNA for me to run the sequences again? Or am I simply reviewing what your lab found?"

"Should be both with no problem. Most of the time, our criminal left enough behind for more than one extra lab to take a look."

"Enough what?" Betty said. She was surprised to finally want to get a look at the data. "Hair? Saliva? Skin cells? I'm guessing the last one included semen."

Willa leaned over and fitted her fingertips into the oval readers built into her briefcase.

"Let me give you the information to look at rather than giving you my inexpert version of the data. One thing I know for sure is the last one did *not* include semen. Our perpetrator was careful. Or wanted us to think so."

She popped the blue case open and rummaged around for a second, then handed a stack of paper to Betty.

"I'll have to figure out where your department gets your paper supplies. So I can invest."

"I know," Willa said, a half smile on her face. "My boss again. In a way, it's good management for a bunch of detectives. Don't trust until you verify, and then verify again. The cloud and the networks are fine. Until they're not."

"Eh, they may have a point. It's bulky and annoying to deal with, but paper does work when the power's out." Betty flipped through several pages. "Your criminal left a hell of a lot of samples for you to work with. Anyone at your lab comment on that?"

"Not the same way you just did."

"What way is that?" Betty said, the old familiar knot back in her chest. What had she just said or done wrong? And what was it going to cost her?

"Suspicious. And in a good way. No one commented, no. They seemed pretty excited to have so much to work with."

"Well sure," Betty said, "this is an embarrassment of riches. Especially with supposedly different people from every single crime scene. Quite a few skin cells, as if every one of them—or your guy—is just getting over a nasty sunburn. Or maybe has a good case of eczema."

Willa stared at Betty, chin in her palm.

"So you're willing to go along with my crazy idea that it's not the boyfriend?"

Betty shrugged. "With the evidence you're finding? So much of it, and all of it pointing to residents of the apartments? I'm willing to go along, look it over, and see what we find. But I have to say your techs made a reasonable assumption even without a full match, Detective."

"Again, they may have. But I don't like the way this feels, especially the assault. And why would so many different people in these buildings steal their own stuff, or report it stolen if they lost it or broke it? Either that, or we have a criminal who never sheds anything that could leave DNA."

"Possible in a few cases," Betty said. "But there are so

many of these. No hair, no fingerprints, no skin cells that appear to come from outside. And so *much* evidence, every time."

She looked up at Willa, trying not to get caught up in where her own mind was wanting to go.

Willa nodded. "You think it's strange, too."

"I think it's worth looking into further. Maybe not by me, but by someone. No matches with your criminal DNA databases?"

"They checked, but by then they'd taken samples from the residents and knew they matched. I'm not sure they looked too hard. But the odds of a criminal having even a partial match with someone who lives in the apartment every time have to be sky high, right?"

"If it's one person, someone who doesn't live there, then yeah. Or your criminal really is that careful to not leave a trace." Betty stopped, an odd tickle floating across her brain.

"What? You see something, it's all over your face."

"Something I can't get ahold of yet. Let me look at what you have first. Do I need to do some kind of swearing in or ritual or donate blood?"

Willa laughed, and Betty was pleasantly surprised at what a full, natural laugh she had.

"I should ask you to do all of the above. But we save that kind of fun for when we have a hidden camera available. My boss might want you to come in at some point for an interview or at least a handshake depending on how this turns out. Other than that, we're good with your application forms there."

"I'll get started then," Betty said. "I'll set up a baseline with my own DNA, then look at whatever you have."

"Your own DNA? What for?"

"It may not look like it, but I run a very careful lab.

Anti-contamination protocols, masks and gloves, scrubbing hands and surfaces before a sequencer run. Even so, things can happen. Just the fact that I'm here all the time and I live upstairs means my genetic material is around. That was part of my work at school, you know."

"Your work with sorting out mixed samples."

"I had the idea to start with the investigator's DNA. Kind of like noise-cancelling headphones, really. One thing to eliminate, to turn the noise down a bit. I stayed in the habit even after... When I'm running my own lab full of wildlife samples, I still get myself tuned out."

Willa stared again, now looking more curious than careful. "Does doing that make your work faster, or better? If you tuned more than one person out?"

"If you mean do I work better with more people in here, absolutely not. If you mean if I block out more than one person's profile, it can help."

"Okay," Willa said. "Tune my profile out, then. Take hair, spit, whatever you need. If I can do anything to help get this solved, I will."

Betty nodded. "That's as good a place as any to get started. You've been here now, and it's possible you're somewhere in those samples. Anyone else you think I should include?"

Willa stared at the floor for a second, shifting her booted foot back and forth.

"No, not right now. We'll see later. Okay?"

Betty got to her feet and stood with her arms crossed.

"Are you trying to test me, Willa? Or trick me? See if I catch some kind of weird loophole you've built in, so you can point out whether I noticed it or not?"

Willa returned Betty's gaze without flinching.

"I am not. That's the last thing I'd do when we need

outside eyes so desperately. You sure don't trust easily. What did they *do* to you at school, Betty?"

"Taught me my charming and endearing habit of never trusting anyone, for one thing. I'll leave it at that for now. Leave whatever you have and I'll get started today."

Chapter 5

Betty paced the floor in her lab two days later, trying her best not to snap at anyone who ventured too near her big black sequencer. The gronking was back after she'd kept it running all weekend long without a rest. Janice the low-rent IT guru had warned Betty several times that the failing cooling fans would only get worse if she didn't let her dig in there and fix them.

And the paranoid (and broke) part of Betty just knew, she *knew* Janice would find a way to junk the whole unit instead of making the repairs. Not because Janice had ever done anything remotely like that.

Mainly because Betty wasn't sure what she'd do without her ancient workhorse.

Jimmy, the part-time secretary, rarely came back into the lab if he could help it. He'd stand in the doorway, toes carefully not on the pea-green tiles, and say his piece from there. Or he'd ask Betty or someone else to meet him in the front office or in the break room.

He stood there now, arms crossed, his ridiculously vintage red golf shirt with the alligator on one side so crisp and neat that Betty wondered if he ironed the thing. One jet black eyebrow was raised, so he was either surprised or feeling put-upon.

"What's up, Jimmy?"

"We have a new contract, with the Baron County Police? And no one thought it necessary to let me in on that?"

Surprised *and* put-upon, then.

"Sorry about that," Betty said, trying not to smile. "That came up over the weekend. You have something against working with the police?"

"No, of course not. That's not much different than piles of digital paperwork from all these state agencies I keep having to deal with. I just wasn't expecting someone from there to call and ask about our payment procedures. I thought you'd managed to get arrested over the weekend, not somehow hustled up a new contract."

"Well, not this *past* weekend. But I can't make any promises about the future. Just give them what they need to know. It's good news, Jimmy. A step up, at least for now."

He scowled, then spoke over his shoulder as he left.

"About time you got the kinds of jobs you deserve. You've been selling yourself and all of us short for too damn long."

The completion chime sounded on the sequencer before Betty could come up with a reply worth following him into his office for.

Both assistants were a bit too focused on their own consoles to have been doing anything but listening in. Betty ignored them and went straight back to her dinosaur machinery.

She leaned into the rounded display that sat on top of the lab bench and studied the screen.

"I'll be damned. This old beauty came through again."

Betty tapped the sequence on the screen to forward everything to her own computer, then scrolled until she found the option for printing. Her assistants jumped at the whir of the printer.

"You're *printing* the results?" said Teesha, dark brown eyes wide, skin nearly as dark startling against her short white coat. "On paper?"

"Yeah, these folks are kind of old school," Betty said. "You should have seen the stack of paperwork I had to sign. Don't worry, I'm sending it electronically, too."

Jose only shook his head, rolled his eyes, and went back to his own row of tiny sample tubes he was filling with yet another set of wildlife samples.

Betty walked over to her laptop, waking the screen just as the results popped up. She fired off a cloud message to Willa, then counted under her breath. She made it to three before her phone buzzed in her pocket.

"You found a pattern," Willa said, her voice low and excited. "Tell me."

"Preliminary, but it looks promising. I'm sure you've heard your lab techs talking about a sample being degraded to differing degrees. Just something that happens at a crime scene or in handling. Well, you sent me what, thirty-seven samples altogether? What do you think the odds are of every single one being degraded to the same degree?"

"All of them? You've got to be kidding me."

"No ma'am. I've never scored many points with my sense of humor, and I'd never joke about this. Degraded down to 82.3%. Every. Single. One."

Willa let out her breath with a loud puff. "From different scenes, on different days, and supposedly from different tenants. Not even within a family or the same apartment. I'd say those odds are long in the extreme. How'd you catch that?"

Betty nodded, scrolling through the individual reports, then remembered she had to talk out loud.

"One reason I'm so attached to my old dinosaur sequencer is I programmed part of her functions myself. Added in analysis subroutines that I could modify for strange things like this. I caught it manually in three of the samples, so I decided to run a quick procedure on all of them. Sure enough, that's a pattern too big to ignore."

"You ready to tell me about your strange theory? The one you couldn't grab the other day?"

"Not yet. Still looking for the words myself. But this big a coordination certainly doesn't make it less likely."

Willa was silent for several seconds.

"I don't want to seem like I'm rushing you, Betty, I truly don't. But could a result like this possibly be natural?

"Assuming the samples weren't tampered with after they were collected, no," Betty said. "They weren't, were they?"

"I'm not going to lie to you. I can't guarantee anything. And I also can't imagine how or why they would have been corrupted once they were in our possession."

"Fair enough. If there was no tampering or mishandling, then again, no. I don't see how this kind of consistent pattern could be natural. Anything new on your end?"

"Nothing new," Willa said. "I suppose that's good news in my line of work most of the time. A little bit frustrating right now. Keep in touch."

Something new happened that same night.

Chapter 6

BETTY FORCED herself to leave the lab only an hour or so after everyone else did. Her father had warned her about the dangers of living not only upstairs from where she worked, but of being the boss who could go in anytime she wanted to. Or stay as late or start as early as her overly motivated nature needed to.

She failed at taking time off in a healthy way most of the time, along with way too many scientists and Americans in general.

Then eventually, she crashed, and even if she didn't actually burn, her brain certainly felt like it did. That usually led to something unpleasant like a nasty case of the flu. A situation that forced her to take it easy.

Once in a while, more and more often the older she got, Betty managed to stop herself before the crash.

Her apartment was hardly palatial or luxurious, but it was nowhere near as outdated or plain as the lab. Big windows situated on opposite walls let in a lovely breeze and pleasant light, and the hardwood floors and pretty blue and yellow kitchen and bathroom tiles actually looked nice in the sun.

She hadn't brought all that much furniture in, but most of it was comfortable and presentable enough for company. When her phone buzzed, Betty was curled up on a brown sectional couch, catching up on a TV show she loved about a different fictional haunted town each season. Absurd, yes, at least to her scientific, logical mind. She'd heard quite a few fans believed the towns and hauntings were real, only disguised to keep them secret.

Betty simply enjoyed the stories.

She groaned when her phone chirped, then bonged like a huge clock tower bell. The alert she'd set for calls she might not want to ignore.

"Damn it, Willa. Tonight of all nights."

Betty took a deep breath and paused the TV show before she answered.

"Got another one?"

"Sorry to disturb you, Betty. I do. *We* do. Two more."

Betty rubbed her eyes, resisting the urge to get up and go downstairs.

"Has this person ever hit two on the same day before?"

"No, but we don't think this is a new pattern. One of the victims was called away on a family emergency for three weeks. I think this was supposed to be discovered sooner."

"Which one are you at?" Betty sat up, now itching to grab the CommuShare train out to Baron County. "Please tell me you're supervising the collection of DNA evidence."

Willa laughed quietly.

"I'm at the one with the person unexpectedly out of town. And you bet I'm watching the collection. One of my most trusted colleagues is watching at the other scene."

"Any chance I can do some of this collection myself?"

Willa answered after a pause.

"Not right now, Betty. I'm sorry. My boss drew the line on that one. Said you'd need to go through training on the latest forensic genetic techniques just like everyone else does."

"Yeah, yeah, too long out of school and dealing with my ancient workhorse equipment and all that. How long does the training take?"

"It takes about six weeks. But the next set of classes doesn't start for another two months. If you still want to by then, I'll do my best to get you signed up. But for now, you're on for reviewing the sequences our techs run, and running your own tests on the secondary samples. Okay?"

Betty sighed, settling back against the cushions.

"Okay. Anything you can tell me about the crime scenes?"

"Well, to the eye it doesn't look much different than any robbery where the criminal either knew what they were after or they didn't want to make much noise. Nothing is thrown around or broken. Drawers are closed, even when things are missing inside them. I'm not going into specifics, but the owner reported jewelry, cash, collectibles, and small electronics missing."

Betty stared at the frozen TV screen.

"No security cameras in these apartments?"

"Wouldn't *that* be nice?" Willa said, and Betty could hear her sneer. "The people who live in these buildings want those in every inch of the lobby and around the outside, too. In maintenance areas, definitely. But they draw the line at the hallways they live down and inside their private spaces. Privacy means more than security, even in modern times when cameras are so easy to program and control."

"Eh, I suppose paranoia is understandable these days. I

have them in my lab spaces, but not in my apartment. Especially since I don't have anything up here anyone in their right mind would want to steal. I'll be waiting for the data and samples. Getting a look at this one that may be three weeks later than intended should be interesting."

"You'll have them as soon as I can get them to you. Now get back to whatever you were doing, as long as it wasn't work. As soon as this scene is finished, I'll be taking my own advice."

Betty ended the call and tapped her fingernails against the phone's screen. What she was thinking was illegal, and certainly immoral. She never would have considered such a thing back in her eager and earnest college days.

But bitter experience then and lean years between now and then had gotten her acquainted with a few fascinating characters. People who might be able to manage things like hacking into the databases of those huge commercial DNA testing companies Betty so disliked.

One of those characters even worked in what might be called legitimate investigations, for an insurance company and all. Which meant totally secure internet connections that happened to be untraceable, too. It was amazing what someone who'd turned her hacker past into a killer new job could get done.

Not tonight, though. Not when Betty didn't even have the new samples in hand. Now if she found the same degradation down to 82.3%, especially with the crime scene that sat undiscovered for three weeks, *that* might be the time.

Betty shook her head, started the TV show again, and did her best to wait patiently.

In this case, her best wasn't very good at all.

Chapter 7

Two days later—well, a bit less since Betty had pretty much slept in her office so she could work the whole time —she stood blinking over her beloved ancient sequencer. The machine had to know how much she loved it, because she'd been telling it so under her breath for the last fifteen minutes.

The hour wasn't nearly as catastrophically late as she'd been known to work, but the broken sleep and growing tension had taken their toll. Betty's feet and back ached, and she had an endlessly irritating twitch in her left eyebrow.

She also had a pretty good idea she was starting to smell a bit too organic for polite company. But some sneaky superstitious corner of her brain insisted if she walked away that long, her workhorse would die of a broken and lonely heart.

"Come on, baby. You know I'd never leave you. No other machine could suit me half as well as you do…"

Intense concentration and weariness combined to produce a hearty yelp out of Betty when the completion chime dinged. Eager as she was, she closed her eyes and let her head drop toward her chest for a few seconds.

Please let it follow the pattern.

Please don't follow the pattern, because what the hell would *that* mean?

She opened her eyes.

82.3% sample degradation in both new crime scenes.

Even in the apartment that had unexpectedly been locked and empty for three weeks.

Betty shook her head and tapped Willa's number.

"You got it?" Willa said.

"82.3. And the sample is a match for the apartment owner."

"Who was out of town when this happened, confirmed. Same things the Baron County techs found. *Now* can you share your great idea?"

Betty paced in a circle around the lab, her shoes squeaking on the tiles.

"What we're finding doesn't make sense, you know that. But what I'm thinking is even worse. Can this somehow be…manufactured? The samples, I mean? Matched up and deposited at the scene?"

"I don't have the slightest idea if that's even possible, Betty. That's why I ask you hard-core science types."

"If you trust your crime scene techs and your lab techs, and I know you do, we're staring at a brick wall. Especially because I'm seeing the same thing. How much subpoena power do you have on this one?"

Willa was silent for long enough that Betty walked another circle around the whole lab.

"It's getting stronger the longer this goes on, but not unlimited. What are you wanting to look at?"

"Records that aren't public record. See if we can get one step ahead of our criminal. Figure out how they're picking their targets. That might lead us to how they're getting access."

Betty heard Willa sigh, long and low.

"My subpoena powers aren't there. Not yet. I can get you access to the regular criminal DNA databases, but that's it. Are *your* powers there yet?"

Betty stopped, staring at the unsettling results on the sequencer's monitor.

"I think they could be nudged that way."

"Low risk?" Willa said.

"So you know as well as I do that *no* risk isn't possible. Somehow that makes me feel better. Yeah, low risk."

"They've been holding an innocent man for sexual assault and murder, Betty. I'm more convinced he didn't do it every day. His name leaked, of course, and that we're holding him because of DNA found at the scene. Now every time another place gets hit, even for robbery, the bloodlust for this poor guy gets worse. If another person gets killed, I guess at least they can't pin that one on him while he's in lockup. But I don't want another person killed."

Betty nodded, already rehearsing the conversation with her friend in her mind.

"Neither do I. Let me ask you one more thing since part of this would be on your side. Is there someone who lives in one of these apartments who might be willing to help us, potentially with a bit of not so low risk?"

"You mean as a target? Bait? Whatever you want to call trying to bring our criminal in where we can grab them?"

"That's what I mean. They don't have to be involved physically, but if my hunch on these records plays out, at least the location and maybe what draws our criminal in might do the trick."

"I have an idea on that. Someone who would help us

and then get out of town for a while, on purpose. He has a sister who I'm quite sure would be willing to donate the DNA and register it to his address, just in case our criminal prefers women. I'm sure enough that I'll say you should go with it when you're ready."

"I've got a few things I can try first, but I'm moving on it."

"Good."

Chapter 8

By the time Betty managed to get in touch with her friend Dana Sanderson, she'd also managed to run several more tests. None of the victims were more than very distantly related. None of them seemed to have any other connection than living in high-end apartments out in Baron County and Maplehurst.

Those apartment complexes weren't owned by the same person or management group. They weren't even rented out by a single agency.

She'd run all the checks of public DNA databases she could manage and the criminal databases Willa got her authorization for, without finding a single hit on any of them.

She'd at least eliminated several of the ways to move forward without getting into this particular low-risk situation. Which of course made the idea even more irresistible.

Dana breezed into the lab at precisely seven that evening as expected, and Betty immediately remembered why she liked Dana so much. Her black pants and jacket with a geeky t-shirt underneath ran awfully close to Betty's own feeble fashion sense.

Her brown hair was shoulder-length and no-nonsense, as was pretty much everything else about her. Unfortunately Dana hadn't brought her best friend and business partner Andre along for this one. Besides bringing his own unique skills and perspective, Andre was miles and miles away from ordinary. The dump could use a good dose of fabulous.

Perhaps most importantly, Dana had a huge laptop bag over one shoulder. Her connection to any place the internet could get her.

Unobserved and unmonitored. Exactly what Betty needed.

She even remembered to turn her own lab security cameras off for the meeting.

"You want me to hack into *what?*" Dana said after the minimal pleasantries were exchanged.

"One of these DNA testing companies. You know, the commercial ones with lots of promises and not a lot to back it up. Several of them if you can manage it."

Dana glanced around the empty lab, focusing on the hulking sequencer last.

"And standing in the middle of your genetics lab, you're honestly asking me this?"

"I know, it sounds kinda nuts. I'll probably see if I can match a couple of things up, but I'm not wanting to read test results or anything like that. At most I want to see if I can find a database that holds samples from more than one of our victims. Narrow down something, anything they all have in common. Then what I'm wanting is to *plant* a test result. A fake one."

Dana scowled at Betty, but she pulled a sleek, black

laptop out of the bag at the same time. She rolled a chair over to one of the empty lab benches.

"You want to catch a criminal by becoming one is what you're telling me."

Betty shrugged. "Yeah, if I have to."

Dana stared intently into Betty's eyes for several seconds, then she nodded.

"Okay, you're serious. You know what you're risking here?"

"I have a pretty good idea. My past isn't exactly squeaky clean, depending on who you ask. What are *you* risking, Dana?"

Dana snorted. "Honestly, not much. I'd never be dumb enough to say this rig is untraceable if someone truly wanted to get to me. I *can* say they'd have to have a good idea what I was doing first. Unless you've already pissed off someone you're not telling me about, that's not likely."

"I'm sure I've pissed off plenty of people that I don't know about, and a few I know all too much about. I don't think there's anyone after me on this, though."

"Good enough for me," Dana said. She flipped open the laptop and pulled out a round black gadget about as big as the palm of her hand. It looked suspiciously like a hockey puck, but most pucks weren't shiny with flashing lights.

"Your direct line to the dark web?"

"Not far from it. I have a secure connection at home and at any of our satellite offices. I don't want to risk going through your WiFi or the regular cellular network for this." She tapped the screen and rattled out several passwords. "What's our first target?"

Betty rolled another chair over, sat with a groan, and stared up at the ceiling.

Biggest one first? One of the obscure ones? Maybe one that no one took seriously?

In the end she went in alphabetical order.

"You got it," Dana said, already typing away.

When an absurdly loud growl made Betty clutch at her stomach, she remembered she hadn't eaten in…she honestly had no idea.

"As you and everyone on the block just heard, I apparently am in need of food. Get you anything?"

"There's supposed to be a great Thai place over at the university that delivers. Andre the professional food snob informed me I'd be a fool if I missed my chance while I'm over here."

Betty laughed. "That's one recommendation I'd never ignore. Coming right up."

Chapter 9

On the third commercial DNA database, with Betty taking over long enough to run her own searches on each one, they finally struck gold. One mailing address match, then another, then another. Every one of the robbery victims had run at least one set of tests there.

Betty hadn't solved the crime, far from it. But Dana had at least given her a place to start seriously looking.

Betty surprised herself and Dana with a big, Thai-food-scented hug.

"You're an absolute genius, Dana."

Thankfully Dana laughed and hugged back instead of pushing her away.

"Well, I'm pretty good at what I do, sure. But this was more you directing my big bad hacker skills than any kind of intuitive leap. I'm hoping this at least points you toward your next move."

Betty spun her chair in a slow circle with one foot, tilting her head from side to side.

"Not sure if it's a great leap, but I do have an idea. You got me in to take a look. Think you can help me plant that fake record? I can get the address and the sample. I just need to be able to put it in the right place."

Dana spun herself around to face Betty, or at least to face her every few seconds when Betty rotated back around.

"I can do that. You thinking you'll be able to draw in your suspect that way?"

"At this point I'm willing to try anything that comes to mind."

Dana nodded, staring around at the lab again.

"You think this person is stealing the samples? From what, a doctor's office or a lab like this one?"

Betty let the chair slow to a stop, shaking her head.

"I don't see how that's possible with the kinds of samples they're finding. It's not just spit or blood. That's what's so strange. They're finding hair and skin cells, and a lot of skin cells. The only way that normally happens is if someone has a bad sunburn or a skin condition."

"And do they? The people being accused?"

"That's the thing. Not one of them has had that kind of chronic problem, going by their appearance and their genome. Whoever's doing this is making it way too damn easy to find DNA to test. It's generally not as simple as walking in and taking a few samples."

Betty got up to pace again, and after a few seconds Dana joined her.

"You don't have to tell me details of the crimes," Dana said. "I understand that. But I'm dying to know what you're thinking this is. What you're pursuing."

Betty glanced at her, wondering how much she could possibly say. An irritating voice in the back of her mind was already starting up a running commentary that was repetitive, but effective.

Chasing phantoms through your own imagination.

Getting science confused with fantasy.

Making a fool of yourself and your education.

And that damn voice sounded way too much like the memory of her most unpleasant former professor for Betty's comfort.

Or for her to allow herself to stop now.

"Okay," she said, "This is going to sound pretty out there. I'm a little amazed I've been thinking it, much less that I'm going to say it out loud."

Dana rolled her eyes. "Did I ever tell you about my first investigation case? The one that got me fired from my old coding job, then got me hired on for what I do now?"

Betty shook her head. She'd wondered about that, a lot. But she'd been too afraid to ask.

"I won't go into the details," Dana said, "but it came down to murder by meditation. I had another that involved candles heated to a certain point before they turned toxic. I never would have believed *any* of that until it happened. So try me with your crazy theory. I respect you and your mind or I wouldn't be here right now."

Betty walked for several more seconds, not sure if she was going to laugh or cry. Someone respecting her mind and saying it right out loud hit her harder than she expected.

She took a deep breath and got it out as fast as she could.

"I think someone is manufacturing the samples and leaving them there to cover their own tracks. I don't see how that's possible, but nothing else makes any kind of sense, so that's where I am."

Before Dana had a chance to say anything, Betty blurted out a question before she could change her mind.

"Did you say murder by *meditation*? Really?"

"You have to let Andre tell you that story. He does a

hell of a lot better job with it than I do. Sounds to me like what you're thinking could be terrifying technology. Not only would we not be able to trust any kind of genetic testing for medical purposes, but everything law enforcement has learned to do with DNA would fall apart."

Betty let her breath out in a whoosh, fighting a sudden urge to curl up on the floor and hide her head. Said out loud, so direct and clear, her idea sounded about a thousand times worse than she'd even been imagining it.

"Yeah, it would. We'd never know if what we had was real or fake. For disaster recovery, or people trying to find family members, or making sure they weren't going to pass along an awful condition like Huntington's Disease. That all goes away, or gets an awful lot less reliable."

"Then we have to figure out who this is and get it stopped. You have your address and DNA information ready?"

Betty hesitated for a second, painfully aware that this was a bright line she wouldn't be able to uncross, no matter how much she might want to in the future.

But the bright line everyone in law enforcement, medicine, so many areas would be forced to cross if they couldn't stop this was a thousand times worse.

"I've got it," Betty said. "Let's get started."

Chapter 10

WHEN HER PHONE buzzed early the next morning, Betty almost managed to dump herself out of her lab chair trying to answer it. She jumped up, waved at her assistants, and all but dashed into her office.

"Willa. You got someone."

"Not exactly, at least I don't think so. No more robberies or hits on the DNA. But we do have someone who has been in all the locations where there *were* robberies. Says he didn't see anything, but he's willing to talk to us."

Betty rubbed her eyes, trying to force her weary brain into some semblance of working order.

"Willing to get his DNA tested?"

"Well, yeah, seems to be. We'll have to do the standard spit instead of hair. He's entirely bald. Skull and face and even eyelashes."

"Alopecia, huh? Or at least he wants us to think so. Close enough, I can work with that. Hold on, did you say he's willing to talk to *us*? Do you mean at the department, or me?"

Willa laughed. "Either one, I guess. Yes, I'm telling you that you can be in on an interview. Secondary, kind of like the samples. I'll do the talking. But I do want your input. A different set of ears, maybe a different set of questions we can work up together before we get started. You up for that?"

"Hell yeah I'm up for that. Just tell me where and when."

"I'll do that. Do you have anything, Betty? From your connection? Your inquires?"

"Not yet. I got everything into place a couple of days ago. I figure it will take time."

"Fair enough. My friend has plans to get out when he needs to, and take his sister with him. We'll get the interview with the HVAC guy set up and let you know."

Betty hung up, already working on several questions in her mind.

THE HVAC GUY turned out to be as anonymous and ordinary as people in such lines of work often were. Brown eyes, medium build, medium skin tone. Several years of living by the motto of get the job done, get out, leave no trace. That kind of constant work requirement seemed to wear down people's edges. Grind them down just enough to fit in.

Face to face with him, and even with his apparent lack of any hair, Betty wondered if she could recognize him passing on the street. His standard issue dark gray pants and light gray button up shirt looked like pretty much every other service person she'd ever seen.

And Jeff Henderson had indeed serviced all of the units

that had had robberies. Though of course, all of his alibis of other appointments seemed airtight.

Sitting across from him and despite all the ordinariness, something about him put Betty on edge. She had the strangest certainty that he was fooling them somehow.

And that he was secretly delighted about it.

His office out in Baron County was boring even by Betty's usual standards. Tan walls, flat tan carpet. Even the speckled acoustic tile ceiling was tan, possibly from a previous occupant's smoking habit. Mr. Henderson's desk was old-fashioned pale green metal, along with the file cabinets.

Sadly the chairs he had for guests came from the same ancient, uninspiring lot. What looked like cushions felt like more steel against Betty's backside. Willa's constant shifting suggested Betty hadn't simply picked the more uncomfortable chair by accident.

She suspected he either frequented Janie's Second Chance Office Emporium or somewhere an awful lot like it.

"So we're agreed that you have serviced the equipment at all the crime scenes," Willa said, firmly in her Serious Detective Mode. "Do you work in other areas besides Baron County?"

"Well sure, as much as I can." Jeff spoke with a bit of a drawl but clipped, as if he was either trying to hide it on purpose or trying to fake it. "Hard to find the kinds of units I'm used to working on out in different parts of town. The latest automated, high-end ones, you know."

"Those seem to be all close together?" Willa said.

Jeff shrugged. "Mostly. Tell you the truth, even the fancy neighborhoods north of the city don't much bother with these. Seems to be mostly in-town, places like Maplehurst and Baron that rich people give a damn about the most efficient units. What they called *green* a long time ago. These were all installed in these units when they were built."

"Kind of like the cameras?" Betty said before she realized she was going to open her mouth.

Willa glanced at her, but didn't say a word.

"Yeah, I guess you could say so, Ms. Falconen. I don't like to judge my clients, mind you. But these folks sure do get excited about having cameras around."

Willa waved her hand toward the ceiling.

"And you don't, Mr. Henderson?"

He shook his head. "Naaaah. Nothing to hide in here, but nothing much worth stealing, either. Got 'em all over my supply warehouse. If I ever brought anything in here that cost more than one of those cameras, I might consider it."

"I'm guessing you feel the same way about giving us a DNA sample," Willa said, giving Betty her cue.

"That's right. Sorry I don't have enough hair left to make it easier on you."

Betty smiled and brought out a syringe sealed in clear plastic, and what looked like a miniature white plastic test tube. She pulled on blue plastic gloves before twisting the lid off the tube with a snap. She handed it over to Mr. Henderson.

"Yeah, I didn't want to be rude," she said, "but can I ask what happened there?"

"Don't know for sure," he said, staring down into the liquid collection medium inside the tube. "Might be that disease that makes all your hair fall out. Might be the wallop of antibiotics I had to take a few weeks back. Had a nasty infection from a cut, got it from an old ventilation system. Doc said it might cause me trouble like this. May or may not ever grow back. To tell you the truth, I've gotten used to it. Kinda nice to not have to fuss with hair."

Betty caught Willa's gaze as she explained to Mr. Henderson how to spit in the vial.

"We're sorry to hear that," Willa said. "To be on the safe side and so we won't have to bother you again, I hope you don't mind giving a blood sample as well."

He flashed a crooked half-grin that did everything but reassure Betty.

She had nothing to go on besides a very strong hunch (so far), but that hunch was screaming that he was nothing he appeared to be.

"Sample away, Ms. Falconen. I want to do everything I can to get this sorted out. I don't much like the idea of my best clients having all these bad things happening to them."

Chapter 11

Betty and Willa had what Willa called the usual post-mortem back in town at The Bean. Betty had to admit the dim, industrial space with exposed ductwork and brick seemed fitting for a post-mortem. Hell, she'd bet half the usual patrons of The Bean would love the idea and proclaim it edgy or some other such nonsense.

Betty could much more easily afford her own with the nice raise she'd gotten for working with Baron County. But she didn't mind one bit when Willa insisted the county would be perfectly happy to pay to keep its best two detectives caffeinated and happy.

"Okay Betty, that was your first official interview. This is your first official order to tell me exactly what you heard and saw. Spill it."

"I seem to remember you were there too," Betty said, strangely reluctant to risk volunteering her impressions.

"I was. And I'm quite sure you remember me saying I wanted a different set of eyes and ears. You're it. Now go."

Betty stared up at the parallel lines of old ventilation ducts, their rounded bulk painted black. She assumed Mr.

Henderson wouldn't let himself be bothered to work on such uninspiring ducts.

"I'll be honest then," she said. "I think he's our guy."

"What, the thief? Or the killer?"

"Both. You asked me. He's hiding something, Willa. Something that makes him so damn happy that he can barely stand to keep it to himself."

Willa sat back and stared at Betty for what felt like an eternity.

"I get the feeling this is going to be a long night," Willa finally said. "Want another?"

"The county still paying?"

"You bet. Even my tight-ass boss is itching to get this one closed, or at least cleared up."

Betty handed her empty cup over and watched Willa walk up and catch one of the jumpy barista's attention right away. Much faster than Betty had ever managed. She wasn't sure if it was Willa's natural charm or the truly scary detective mode.

Betty shook her head, leaning forward and tangling her fingers up in her hair.

Yeah, that detective mode. Betty was scared to death Willa was about to engage it, only with Betty in the spotlight rather than their suspiciously ordinary HVAC guy.

And being in any kind of spotlight wasn't Betty's favorite thing by a long shot. One of the many reasons she rapid-cycled between wanting to catch whoever was doing all this and regretting she'd ever gotten involved.

A thump on the table a bit louder than the low murmur of conversation and the regular hiss of the espresso machine got Betty to look up. Willa sat across from her, and two steaming cups of coffee waited.

"Go ahead and ask whatever you're going to," Betty said, pulling her coffee close so she could breathe in the heavenly aroma. "I may not be a detective, but I don't need to be with the way you're looking at me."

Willa nodded. "You're right. You're not a detective. But you're showing me pretty clear signs of some kind of cop instinct with this Henderson guy. Did your forensic genetics studies ever go as far as interrogation training? Classroom or fieldwork?"

"Nope. I thought about that when I was an undergrad, but it never fit into my schedule. By the time I got to grad school, I was too caught up in the genetics side to fit it in. I never got back around to it before I got out."

"Fair enough," Willa said. "Though I have to say you'll have the chance to get that interrogation training if you decide to get into the department's forensic genetics training. And I'll say you *should* do that. Now, what makes you so sure he's the one? That he could actually sit across from us and lie so easily?"

Betty closed her eyes for a second, and her mind and her gut shifted a lot closer to *never should have gotten involved*. But even so, she knew it was too late to get up and walk away now.

"You know, I couldn't have said why until just now. He reminded me of someone. From my past. Unless my memory is failing or humans have changed dramatically in a short amount of time, he's lying through his teeth and delighted about whatever he's getting over on us."

Willa rubbed at her temples, then stared at Betty. The Serious Detective had just returned.

"Someone from your past. Are we talking your academic days, or before or after then?"

Betty sipped her coffee even though she knew trying to buy time was useless.

"Near the end of my academic days. I've run across a few people since then who get a little too excited about seeing exactly how much they can get away with. But no one else ever came close."

"You went to school in Michigan, right?"

"Surely you knew that from my squeaky clean background checks, Willa."

"I did, yeah. This is the part of interrogation that I call thinking out loud, because I know the subject. And in this case, she knows where I'm headed with all this. Doesn't she?"

Betty raised her chin and met Willa's intense gaze. All the noise and sights and smells of The Bean passed unnoticed around them. Betty couldn't quite stop the shiver that ran along her spine.

"I have a good idea where you're headed," Betty said. "Now you answer a question for me, Detective Belladeux. Is this going to get us closer to locking our criminal up? If you tell me it is, then I'll have to trust you when it comes to digging around where I'd rather not go."

"What I'm after right this second is protecting our investigation, yes. Making sure nothing blows up in our faces later on. Okay?"

"Okay. Ask what you need to."

Willa tapped her official Baron County credit card on the table, then looked up at Betty.

"This thing in your past. Is it going to cause us trouble here? With the investigation?"

Chapter 12

BETTY STARTED to shake her head, then stopped. She'd been trying to do that with this situation for years, even while it weighed her job, her career, her life down like a gigantic anchor. But by pretending it either hadn't happened at all—or maybe worse, that it hadn't affected her—all she was doing was covering for someone else's shitty behavior.

"I don't know, Willa. I honestly don't know. I didn't expect to get hit in the gut with it, not like this. I know that's not the answer you or your boss need. I'm sorry."

Willa sat back and crossed her arms, and Betty's blood ran cold.

"Then I'm afraid your time has run out," Willa said. "I know nothing showed up on your background checks, or your academic records for that matter. Yet it sounds like you've lived pretty much your whole adult life in fear of whatever happened. You know how much is at stake here. I can't prepare my boss, myself, or this investigation until I know what to prepare for."

Betty closed her eyes, trying to imagine walking out of

here without the burden of secrecy she'd carried for someone else for all these years. What would that even feel like, to get it out to even one person?

What would she base the rest of her life on?

She had to be willing to find out.

"Okay. I want this asshole caught, you understand. Badly. But this isn't going to be easy for me. But I'll do my best." Betty finished her coffee and took a deep breath.

"I had a faculty mentor during the first year of my master's, one of those mentors undergrads compete tooth and nail to get. It was a serious coup for me to land her. The key to my entire career, that kind of thing. I didn't sit back and expect smooth sailing. I'm not made like that, as you well know. But I thought the path might get a little bit less turbulent with her showing the way."

"And it didn't," Willa said.

"It seemed to, at first. She was nothing but encouraging. Positive. Pushed me when I needed it, made me take the praise when I tried to back away. Just what I needed in other words. The first year went like that, me gradually gaining more confidence. In myself and in her."

"What changed?"

"At the time and for a long time after, I thought what changed was I got cocky. Decided I'd made it and I didn't need her or anyone else to show me the way. Like I'd found the secret decoder ring or some other such bullshit, and even having an advisor was another waste of my time."

"And now?"

"I've worked with enough young lab geeks to get an idea how they behave. Good and bad. Now I think it *was* that I didn't need her. But not because I got cocky. Because I realized I was skilled on my own. I'd not only gotten myself there without her help, but I'd started to…surpass her. To move in directions she wasn't able to go. Or maybe that she was afraid to go. That broke the spell for me, and she knew it."

"Let me guess," Willa said, leaning forward. "That turned you into a threat."

"Got it in one. These things happen outside of academia, huh?"

Willa rolled her eyes and smiled, but the smile wasn't a happy one.

"More than I want to think about in my line of work. She caused you trouble then? With the other faculty, or the board, whatever directs the programs?"

Betty shook her head, not even trying to smile.

"That I probably could have handled and gotten through. Well, I did get through, but I might have had a hell of a lot fewer bruises. There were other professors who would have been happy to mentor me. Once I started to get attention for my work, got brave enough to put it out there, that wasn't a problem. The problem was when *she* started putting my work out there."

"She claimed your work as her own?"

"She certainly used huge parts of it as a foundation. Claimed I'd developed my methods of sorting out mixed DNA samples under her close guidance, that I wouldn't have even started down that path otherwise. The truth was I did all of that work off on my own. I didn't really think about the reason then, other than wanting to be certain I had it right before I let anything get out. But now I think I was already starting to distrust her. So I kept all of those projects to myself."

"What happened?"

"I bucked the system, and it kicked back harder. I took my suspicions to the dean of our department. But I had no way to know—and I never would have suspected—that she'd already done that. She pretty much accused me of doing what *she* did. Of poaching off her work and passing it off as my own. She had the dean convinced I'd come in and make these claims, and of course I walked right into it."

Betty sat back and stared up at the overhead ductwork again. Getting the words out wasn't quite as hard as she'd expected. But she didn't exactly feel relieved just yet.

"I'd broken the rule of ratting out one of their own," she said. "They weren't going to stop me from graduating, not with the noise my work was already making. Looked good for the department no matter who claimed it. But they weren't going to recommend me for jobs, internships, anything else. They were willing to do whatever it took to get me out of there and shut me up. And I shut up. It got so bad there at the end, Willa, I more than halfway believed them. I halfway believed I *had* stolen the ideas and the tech and the work"

"They gaslighted you."

"Maybe. They definitely broke down the confidence I'd worked so hard to build. Partly because she'd helped me do that. She knew where the weaknesses were. Exactly where to poke and prod. And where to put the knife."

"Do you know where any of the rest of them are now?"

"Besides her, not really. She did the most harm, I guess. Made the biggest impression. She's still at the same school, department head now. I think she figured if she got herself built up enough, in contact with enough people, they'd believe her over everyone she accused, or who accused her. She was pretty much right in the few cases where I gave them the chance to get to me."

Willa sighed, her lips compressed into a thin line.

"And that's how you ended up here," she said. "In a lab that's not even close to up to your skills. Doing work that pays the bills, more or less. Letting one of the best minds to ever have an interest in forensic DNA analysis rot without anything to actually do."

Betty only nodded. She might not like what Willa was saying, but there was no real rational way to dispute any of it.

"That about brings us up to speed," Betty said. "As far as hurting the investigation, that all depends on how much pull she still has left in the field. Whether she has enough interest and power to accomplish something or just wants to run her mouth. I'm just guessing here, but from what I remember, she'd have to have found a whole string of oh-so-promising grad students to manipulate and steal from to keep herself relevant. She may very well have done just that."

"That's something I can look into," Willa said, "and with your blessing I will. My guess from my own experience is she either kept finding those students or she got close enough to getting caught at some point that she forced herself to stop. Since she stayed on where she was and even advanced, I'd bet she figured out a much better way of keeping her head down and making sure nothing else got out. I'll figure that out."

Betty closed her eyes and nodded, surprised that she finally did feel better.

"I appreciate that. Either way it turns out, I'm sorry, Willa. I should have told you about all of this sooner. Probably before you got all wrapped in working with me to begin with."

Willa smiled, and not her chilling Serious Detective smile. This was the smile of a friend who actually gave a damn about a bad thing happening, even years ago.

"We couldn't have gotten half this far or nearly this fast without you. You might have kept yourself underground and off her radar every bit as much as you wanted to, you know. She might not even try to get involved. If she tries to cause trouble, we'll deal with it. Right now let's focus on our HVAC guy's samples and go from there."

Betty's DNA trap made a catch before anyone else could cause trouble.

Chapter 13

A FEW DAYS LATER, Betty wasn't sure if she appreciated having company in her lab or missed her solitude late at night more.

Another robbery out in Maplehurst—the same address as the fake record Dana helped Betty plant in the commercial database—brought both Dana and her ultra-secure laptop. Willa did her best not to show it, but being relegated to pacing and waiting for the other two to finish did not suit her the least bit well.

Betty admitted, at least to herself, that she was a bit disappointed that neither Dana nor Willa asked too many questions of each other. Not only would that have been entertaining, but it would have kept both of them from focusing on her.

All three sipped from Betty's secret coffee stash rather than heading out to The Bean. She figured Dana deserved it for helping make the DNA plant in the first place. And Willa for livening up Betty's life considerably.

If this kind of excitement—and steady, well-paying work—kept up, Betty might upgrade her gronking workhorse someday after all. For now, she waited, absently patting the hulking sequencer from time to time. If the poor thing was ever going to give it all up and quit, having Dana's sleek laptop working a few feet away might do it.

"You're sure it's our sample?" Willa said again. "The one you planted?" Her sock feet were silent on the lab's pea-green tiles, and the bright yellow hue of the socks were a shocking contrast to her black pajamas.

"Exactly the same sample and address," Betty said.

Willa stopped on the other side of the high white lab table from Betty and Dana, hands on her hips.

"Why are you processing it, then? I don't understand. I get why Dana's running the trace to try to see who accessed it. But won't the crime scene DNA sample be the same as the one you planted?"

Betty pressed her hands against the small of her back and stretched. She was getting too old for this all-night bullshit.

"Remember the degradation we've seen in the other samples?"

"Of course I do. 82.3%."

"That's part of it, to make sure we have the same source that's been working in the apartments. Whatever they're doing to end up with the same numbers on each sample, we want to make sure this isn't something new. I'm checking to see if they cleaned up the sample at the same time. I planted a false sequence, a string that makes no sense. And hell, I need something to do while Dana here works."

Dana shook her head without looking up from her laptop's screen. Her magic sparkly hockey puck of an internet connection blinked away on the table beside her.

"Ask me to hack into a commercial DNA database to plant a fake record, *then* to trace back and see who accessed the fake. *And* expect me to do it in what, a few minutes? I might just keep Andre's next restaurant recommendation to myself."

Betty laughed at Willa's puzzled expression.

"Trust me, Willa. That's a sincere and serious threat. Andre's a hell of a lot better connected than the three of us combined. Much better taste, too."

Betty switched the sequencer's view to the second sample she was running right now. Old as her beloved machine was, it was more than capable of working with more than one sample without losing speed. She switched back at the sound of the completion chime.

"I'll be damned," she said under her breath. Willa and even Dana stood close enough behind her that she felt their warmth in the cool lab. "Smart as our criminal may be, they didn't bother to look too closely at the DNA they were stealing. My nonsense sequence is right there, plain as day."

Dana grunted as she moved back over to her own machine.

"And the testing service didn't catch it either? You may be right about their quality control, Betty."

Betty continued to scroll through the results screen, her eyes darting over the letters and numbers, reflexively looking for patterns.

"Not even I can blame that one on the commercial database. They never actually received a sample. We *put* the results there. So they never tested it. And if they had, they wouldn't have been looking for the 82.3% deterioration that I just now spotted."

"So that means our target simply lifted what you left for them," Willa said, pacing again. "And assumed the address was legit. But how the hell did the fake DNA end up back at the address for us to find? And like you say, Betty, there was a hell of a lot of it."

Dana gasped, then slowly turned to face Betty and Willa.

"Another question might be how—and why—someone at the same address accessed that commercial database. A couple of weeks ago, right after we planted it."

"The same place?" Betty spoke at the same time Willa said: "From inside the apartment?"

"Afraid so. This trace gets back to the internet trunk in Baron County, then the apartment complex. You gave me data about the computers in that apartment, remember? This is the MAC address for one of those. The identifier for that specific machine. Whoever broke into the commercial database to get our sample was in the same place."

Willa sat heavily in one of the lab assistant's chairs, rubbing at her face.

"And we're back to the refusal to have damn cameras in the hallways or the apartments themselves. And not much else."

"We know it's someone local, right?" Betty said. "Can you tell if they were in front of the computer, Dana? Or could they have been somewhere else but using it?"

"The data doesn't seem to go anywhere else, and it's not a laptop. Not nearly as big as your antique under there, but not portable. I'd bet sitting right there."

All three of them jumped at the sequencer's second completion chime.

"What else were you running?" Willa said.

Betty was silent until Willa asked again, too afraid of making a mistake to want to speak.

"This is our friendly and extremely ordinary HVAC tech," Betty said. "Jeff Henderson."

"Don't tell me he's a match," Dana said.

"Oh no, he's not a match. Not for any of the genes related to alopecia, for one thing."

"You *said* he was lying," Willa said. "I bet I can get his medical records to check on the antibiotic thing he claimed."

Betty turned in her chair, shaking her head.

"You can do that if you want. But that's not the most interesting thing about Mr. Henderson's sample. The most interesting thing is 82.3%."

Dana looked confused, but Willa's eyes widened.

"You have got to be shitting me."

"No, Detective Belladeux, I assure you I'm not. Before either of you get rude enough to ask, I have checked the calibration on my lovely workhorse sequencer. That result is legitimate. And exactly the same as all our other crime scene DNA samples."

Now Dana scowled and leaned in closer for another look.

"I'm guessing everything at Baron County's facilities has been calibrated, too," Dana said. "And didn't you collect the HVAC guy's sample yourself, Betty?"

This time Betty got up to pace.

"I did. Spit and blood. There's no way it deteriorated that much when it came straight from his freaking vein."

"So now what?" Willa said. "I know how this sounds, but we can't be saying his *blood* is somehow fake, right?"

Betty stood across the table in the same spot Willa had taken before, drumming her fingers on the surface.

"I don't see how. DNA doesn't lie. But I'd never imagined I'd see all these samples that don't make any sense, either. Something is off here and we're missing it."

Dana stared up at the ceiling. "You said you had his spit and blood. And that he didn't show any of the common genes for alopecia. I know this is out there, but is he getting rid of his hair for this very reason? To make sure you can't get an ongoing record?"

Betty leaned forward, elbows on the table now.

"I guess he could be, but why? Some kinds of gene therapy can cause a weird result, maybe, but why hide like this? And how the hell are we going to find out?"

Willa nodded to herself, still staring at the sequencer's display.

"This might be a long shot," she said, "and a stretch depending on what kind of mood my boss and the judge are in. But I can see about getting a court order for new samples. More *private* samples, maybe. Hair he might not be so easily inclined to remove."

"You don't mean his pubic hair," Dana said, but she was grinning.

Willa giggled. "I most certainly do. Whoever we're dealing with has been smart enough to stay out of our reach so far. But they messed up by not catching that fake sequence, right Betty?"

"They did. And if it is our HVAC guy and he still has his hair down there, it might be long enough to analyze and go back for several months. It's worth a shot, I say."

Willa had her smartphone out and tapping away already.

"He's an independent contractor, so I don't trust his records. But I do trust the maintenance records of the building managers for those apartments. I should know by tomorrow whether Jeff Henderson was in the neighborhood around the time of the robberies. And the murder."

Chapter 14

Despite all the trouble she'd gone through trying and mostly failing to get credit for her own work all those years ago, Betty had never been more grateful to be able to sort out mixed DNA samples. She'd never expected to put them to use in such odd—she would say impossible—circumstances.

Turned out Jeff Henderson wasn't scheduled to work in any of the apartments the day they were robbed, just like he'd said. But he was in each building the day before every single one. Building managers desperate to get the robberies stopped and avoid another murder were more than happy to provide blueprints.

Blueprints that revealed ductwork and crawlspaces easily large enough for Jeff Henderson to squeeze through.

Another thing Betty was grateful for as she, Willa, and Dana once again waited on her priceless and beloved sequencer to finish processing?

She hadn't been there when the rather private hair she was analyzing was collected. Turned out Mr. Henderson was suddenly not so willing to cooperate with the investigation once he understood what the court order required. The sample had been acquired while he was in Baron County police custody, where he remained days later.

For once, Betty didn't want to know more.

But Willa was more than happy to share exactly how the little bundle of dark, curly hair was separated from his body. In fact, she was eager to. And Dana supplied the perfect enthusiastic audience to keep the tale going.

This time they all huddled close to the sequencer in Betty's lab rather than anyone pacing. A loose plan to go out for a nice dinner rather than ordering takeout yet again had everyone dressed in casual but presentable clothes. Blue jeans, blouses or button up shirts.

Betty suspected she wasn't the only one who would rather troop up to her apartment when this was finished, gather round the TV for a few hours of her favorite haunted town show, and try yet another delivery place instead.

"You didn't go in there by *yourself?*" Dana said, clutching a mug of Betty's secret coffee. "Please tell me you're smarter than that."

"I'm smarter than that," Willa said, rolling her eyes. "We already knew our guy was lying about something, and that he'd been at every single crime scene. I had three deputies with me. The weird thing was this guy didn't even seem surprised to see us, you know? Like he'd been waiting for someone to show up to drag his ass in."

Dana shivered and shook her head. "I had one like that, a former co-worker who I never could stand. Caught him helping himself to an absurd amount of the company's money from the outside. I swear he was relieved it was over."

"Was yours like that?" Betty said, interested despite herself.

"*Ours*, you mean? No, not relieved. More resigned. He opened the door, nodded once, and said he'd be right back. Our warrant specified he was a flight and personal harm risk, so the deputies went right in after him. He'd gone straight to his refrigerator, and they caught him with a syringe held to his jugular vein if you can believe that."

Betty turned away from her sequencer to stare at Willa.

"What was in the syringe? The virus?"

"No, but we did recover a few more syringes we could analyze. I'll get back to that. What he'd grabbed for himself was a toxin, nasty one, too. If he'd been quick enough—or maybe if he'd had the guts—he would have been dead before we could have gotten him to any kind of hospital. As it was, the deputies hit him with the freeze-field and took him down."

"Is that when you got it?" Dana said with a faint trace of a smile. "The hair?"

Willa shook her head. "I didn't get it, though if he's our guy, I'd be happy to yank every last hair out myself. The deputies hauled him in and collected the sample at the jail while he was still out. The way he tried to take himself out and what we found justified the collection quite nicely. From what the deputies told me, Jeff Henderson or whoever he really is didn't have the slightest bit of hair loss in the…region."

Betty glanced at the remaining samples, all sealed inside clear plastic envelopes. She'd been happy to use gloves and every other precaution she could think of, more to avoid touching the material for once rather than worrying about data integrity.

Neither she, Dana, or Willa jumped when the sequencer chimed out its accomplishment. Betty thought they were all too weary and tense to manage something as energetic as jumping.

"That looks..." Willa said, squinting at the screen, "jumbled. All mixed together."

"It is," Betty said. "I've never seen anything like it. If I didn't know the source, if I hadn't put the single hair in myself, I would have been convinced we were looking at a contaminated sample. Or just one from a busy environment where a bunch of people left DNA."

"But we're not looking at that," Dana said.

"No. We're looking at one hair that carries several genomes. Seventeen to be exact. I've heard of rare cases where a twin was reabsorbed in the womb, and that left two different genotypes in different organs. Odd results from bone marrow transplants. Again, with two results. But nothing in nature or medicine that I know of behaves like this."

"All those genomes," Willa said. "Any of them happen to match our crime victims?"

"I haven't compared them yet," Betty said, "but I will. And I'll bet we'll find your matches. I still don't know how that's possible, but there's no way this is some kind of natural occurrence."

"You mentioned gene therapy the other day," Dana said. "Could it still be something like that? Some kind of vaccine or virus or whatever that makes his body produce different DNA?"

Willa smiled, but the look of it chilled Betty to the bone.

"That's part of what I meant about getting back to the other syringes. We just got those results this morning. It was a virus, yes. Engineered to force his body to excrete another genome, but not to change his appearance. Skin cells, saliva, even blood for a while. Hair too, which is why he got rid of it. That's not the disturbing part, though."

"I'm not sure I want to hear the disturbing part, then," Betty said. She was afraid she already knew.

"I didn't either," Willa said. "But I would have reported this to you even if you were strangers. He had one typed to my genome. One to yours, Betty. And one to yours, Dana."

Betty shivered, not the least bit happy at being proven right. Dana's wide eyes and flushed cheeks showed she wasn't doing much better.

"How the hell did he *know*?" Dana said.

"Might not have been him at all." Willa rubbed her upper arms. "There's no indication he has the facility or the skills to design the virus. Only the willingness to inject himself with it, then walk into all these people's lives. I'm hoping we can figure out who did make it, though. Who's pulling this guy's strings."

"I'll do whatever I can to help with that," Betty said. "After everything he's done and apparently wanted to do, I'm not happy letting someone even worse get away. Let me run the search for matches from the crime scenes. We'll figure the rest out, I promise."

"I'm in too, you know that," Dana said. "I'm not about to let this whole thing start up again, here or anywhere else But we *got* this one, Willa. He's even behind bars already thanks to you."

"Thanks to both of you," Willa said. "And thanks to your ancient sequencer here. I know you want to upgrade the processor and the memory, and you probably should. But you can't ever get rid of her."

Chapter 15

Betty kept her word to Willa, and herself, by finally calling in Janice, her low-rent IT guru. But not until she compared Jeff Henderson's samples against all the crime scene samples.

Matches for every apartment burglary, with the band of DNA on his rather personal hair changing in the same order as when the break-ins happened. Except for one.

The sample from the apartment where the owner had unexpectedly been out of town for weeks was in the wrong order in the DNA sequence.

The other surprise was the sample that showed up in Mr. Henderson's hair at the same time the woman was assaulted and murdered.

Rather than matching a neighbor or her boyfriend, that sample matched the victim. So if he was extremely careful and used protection, the only traces that would show up under the victim's fingernails, in her mouth or teeth, or anywhere else on her body would be her own.

That somehow made the whole business even more loathsome.

The Baron County lab found hits on the other bits of DNA that matched other robberies in the area. Enough to put Mr. Henderson away for a long, long time. Even with all that, he refused to name who'd supplied him with the injections that forced his body to produce genes that weren't his own.

He refused to give his real name or any other information about himself. So he was currently cooling his heels in the Baron County Jail, waiting for his body to shed the virus and produce his own DNA. And for his hair to grow out long enough to do the same.

Betty was doing her best not to hover over Janice and the sad-looking innards of her beloved sequencer when Willa walked into the lab. Betty had sent everyone else home for the day, mainly because she knew she'd snap at at least one of them if they stayed.

Only a little bit because she was afraid they'd distract Janice while she worked.

Willa was dressed quite a bit more formally than when Betty saw her last. The silky black pajamas were gone, replaced by a smart blue pantsuit. Her usually messy hair was photo-shoot neat. She carried the same thick blue metal briefcase she'd brought what felt like years ago but was only a few weeks.

Betty surprised herself by giving Willa a great big hug. Willa's wide eyes and huge grin proved she'd been pleasantly surprised.

"Detective Belladeux, how kind of you to drop by," Betty said. "I know Janice and my sequencer appreciate the attention and concern."

Janice looked up from her crouch on the pea-green tiles, swinging her streaked purple and green hair out of her eyes. She was dainty enough to seem dwarfed by the hulking machine, but confident and steady enough that

Betty wasn't all that worried by the vast array of strange parts that surrounded her.

Not *too* worried, anyway.

"Are you the reason Betty's finally letting me upgrade this heap?" Janice said.

"I'm proud to say yes I am," Willa said. "That heap helped solve a whole lot of crimes over the past month."

Janice waved one hand—her short nails alternating purple and green to match her hair—at the scattered bits of technology.

"It certainly has…endured for a long time. I'll have everything running better than ever by the end of the day."

Betty smiled, hoping her paranoia didn't show through.

"What's up, Willa? I'm glad to see you, but I thought you were in court today?"

Willa thumped the briefcase onto one of the lab tables and flipped it open. She handed a stack of papers to Betty.

"Oh, I was in court all right, and other places. Brought a few things you might be interested in. First of all, remember how I told you the next forensic genetics training classes didn't start for a couple of months? Well, that's right around the corner now. If you're still interested, Baron County would be delighted to pick up the bill."

Betty stared at Willa for a second, then rubbed her temples. She was really trying to hide the tears that had sprung up, and not very successfully.

"That would be…wow. Thank you, Willa. Thank you so much."

Willa laughed. "See if you still want to thank me when you're drowning in even more paperwork than my boss produces on a daily basis. You'll wish you were back in academics." She handed over another stack of papers, this one embossed with the seal of the court. "On the subject of academics…"

"I have no idea what you're giving me," Betty said, scowling at the documents. "Something to do with intellectual property?"

Willa sat beside Betty and flipped a few of the pages back.

"I'm sure this will make perfect sense once it all sinks in. What you have there is verification from your former professor and advisor that you, and only you, developed the methods of sorting and sequencing multiple samples of DNA. Along with transfers for any patents related to those methods. Once we get your signature on a few items, she'll be remitting the income she never actually earned in the first place. Last are letters of commendation and recommendation from her and those she misled about you years ago, should you ever need those to seek employment."

Betty blinked, trying to force her brain to focus and run those words back again.

Those impossible words.

"How did you do this, Willa? How?"

Dana popped her head through the door, then strolled into the lab. She was more dressed up than usual, too, wearing an actual skirt and a lovely red blouse.

"I might have helped a bit. It seems your former advisor has made quite a habit of…shall we say *borrowing* the hard work of her students. You weren't the first, Betty. And you weren't the last. But she has now seen the error of her ways. All it took was a careful audit of her computer systems."

Dana and Willa stood shoulder to shoulder, smiling.

"And a quick conversation with a member of the law enforcement community," Willa said. "She was remarkably cooperative in the end."

Betty looked from one to the other, not sure what to do or say. She was afraid if she waited too much longer, she'd start boo-hooing on the spot, and Janice would never let her live that down.

"Your subpoena powers have certainly grown, Detective Belladeux," Betty said. "And I think you've far surpassed the hacking skills of your youth, Dana."

Willa and Dana smiled at each other before they turned back to Betty.

"I guess something about working with you brings out the best in us," Dana said.

"Sure does," Willa said. "I think that something is called friendship. I say we leave your IT guru to work in peace and head out for that long-overdue celebratory dinner."

ABOUT KARI

A biology and genetics nerd since she first read about Gregor Mendel and his pea plants, Kari Kilgore's wanderlust and imagination lead her all over the world on grand adventures. Her heart and family bring her home to her native Appalachian Mountains of Virginia. From that solid base, she and her husband Jason A. Adams bring those adventures to life in fiction.

Kari writes science fiction, fantasy, and horror, and she's happiest when she surprises herself. She lives at the end of a long dirt road in the middle of the woods with Jason, various house critters, and wildlife they're better off not knowing more about.

The Confidential Adventure Club

For Kari's exclusive free After The End stories and deleted scenes, discounts, early pre-sale releases, adorable pet photos, and a whole lot more not available anywhere else, pay a visit to The Confidential Adventure Club at www.smarturl.it/c-a-club.

Hope to see you there!

www.karikilgore.com
www.spiralpublishing.net

ALSO BY KARI KILGORE

I hope you enjoyed reading *DNA Never Lies* as much as I enjoyed writing it. Betty Falconen's next mystery adventure is on the way with Bending the Code ∞ Book Two, with more to come.

Dana and her fabulous best friend Andre also have several stories with more on the way, starting with their introduction in *The Sound of Murder*. Be the first to know about release dates and check out more of my fiction at www.karikilgore.com.

The Confidential Adventure Club

Want more fiction from Kari, including stories, discounts, and box sets not available anywhere else? Want to hear about locations, research, and other cool things that inspired this story and beyond? Want all that and adorable pet photos, too?

Join The Confidential Adventure Club and get a thank you gift of a free short story and a whole lot more at www.smarturl.it/c-a-club.

Hope to see you there!

The Storms of Future Past Series:

Dreaming the Storm

Joining the Storm

Into the Storm

Fighting the Storm

Sensing the Storm: A Storms of Future Past Prequel Story

Storms of Future Past Books One through Four Collection

The Voices through Time Series:

Songs in the Mountain

Secrets in the Land

Walking the Ghosts: A Voices through Time Novella

Dispatches from the Galaxy Stories:

Restricted Species

The Becalmed

The Garbage Belt

Terminalia Short Stories:

Terminalia

Little Five

Novels:

Until Death

The Dream Thief

Hand Me Downs

Novellas:

Legacy of the Land

In the Pines

Collections:

Fantastic Women: A Dark Fantasy Novella Trio

Fantastic Shorts: Volume 1

Near Future Forward (with Jason A. Adams)

Fantastic Shorts: Volume 2

Short Stories:

Intentions, The Seeds of Love, Wicked Bone, The Sound of Murder, Reflections, The Last Dragonkeeper, The Earworms, Odds and Endings, Dawn Visitor, The Spider Who Ate the Elephant

www.ingramcontent.com/pod-product-compliance
Lightning Source LLC
Chambersburg PA
CBHW032042180726
48284CB00008B/2711